CARSON'S ZOO ADVENTURE

A LESSON ON LOVE

WRITTEN BY T.O. MOORE
ILLUSTRATED BY HAILEY CAMPBELL

First Printing: 2020

ISBN: 978-1-7334913-4-1

LCCN: 2020941965

Scripture quotations are from The ESV® Bible (The Holy Bible, English Standard Version®), copyright © 2001 by Crossway, a publishing ministry of Good News Publishers. Used by permission. All rights reserved.

For more information about this book or other grassleaf works, please visit grassleafpublishing.com or email grassleafbooks@gmail.com. Also, be sure to search grassleaf Publishing on Amazon to view our entire library of works.

To my husband, Lamar, thank you for your unconditional love.

To my children (Carson & Gracyn), my nieces (Crysten, Carmynn, Chloe, and Harper), and my nephew (Noah)—always seek to show love to all people. - T.O. Moore

This is dedicated to the children who embrace their differences, value those who are different from them, and understand that these differences are what make them special, amazing, and unique. - Hailey Campbell

'm **so** excited to take a family trip today to my **favorite** place, the **ZOO.**

On the
car ride there, I
imagine all of the
wonderful animals
I will see.

As I gaze out the window,

I even begin to see

animals

in the

clouds.

Wow!

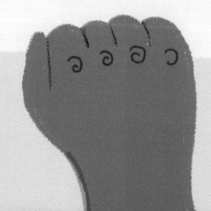

we drive for what seems like **days**

before stopping on the side of the road

to **help** another family.

"Daddy, why did you stop and help those strangers?"

"well Carson, they are a family like us, trying to have a fun day together. Always **show love and help others** when you can."

ZOO   EN

After our small delay,
we finally arrive
at the ZOO.

TRANCE

I rush inside
to spot
all of my
favorites.

There are **tall** animals with extremely long necks and **small** animals that move very *quickly*.

See animals swinging from tree to tree

and animals swimming in deep, blue water.

I am **amazed** at all the different kinds of **animals**.

As my Mommy hastens us along to gather for the **tiger** show, I notice a little girl crying hysterically.

TIGER SHOW
this! way!

She is sad that her

  balloon animal **POPPed** as she

scuffled along in the zoo.

Aha! **This** has to be what my Daddy was talking about!

With my parents' permission, we find the **talented** balloon man and quickly return to the sad, little girl.

Right there on the spot,
the **kind** balloon man
constructs an original creatio
for my new **friend**, Olivia.

She is so **thankful** and **happy** to have a pretty flower balloon.

As we walk
to the car

after an
adventurous day,

Daddy asks,
"Son, why
such a big smile"

I exclaim,

"Daddy, I am very happy!"

with a look of satisfaction,

Daddy responds,

"That is because you showed **love** to that little girl. It feels good when you express love and treat people **right**."

"carson, always try to find a **small** way to make a **big** difference. Keep up the great work by continuing to show **love**."

"I am proud of you, Son."

Reflection Questions

"But the fruit of the Spirit is **love**, joy, peace, patience, kindness, goodness, faithfulness, gentleness, self-control...If we live by the Spirit, let us also keep in step with the Spirit." - Galatians 5:22-23;25

As the author, my hope is that you use this section of the book as a way to make practical connections for your young reader. The reflection questions are meant to build a bridge between the characteristic (love) and real life.

1. What is love?
2. How do you know when people love you? What do they do to show you love?
3. How does it make you feel when you are loved?
4. What are some ways you can show love to others?

A note about Grassleaf Publishing

Grassleaf Publishing was created because of the belief that good literary works, films, music, and art of all types can come from anywhere and anyone. After all, all goodness comes from He who created goodness, and He is powerful enough to display that goodness through any individual.

Grassleaf Publishing is as much a ministry as it is a business. That's why your support means so much. Our focus is to impact the lives of others and the world in which we live, not to maximize profits. Certainly, it takes money to produce our works, but we also are mindful to balance that necessity with generosity.

At Grassleaf Publishing, it is believed that good books can still be written. But the process of publishing must evolve. That's why Grassleaf operates differently than the traditional publishing company. Content and quality are the sole focus. The status, background, or life experience of an author doesn't matter. Grassleaf Publishing believes that if good content is made available, He will see that it serves its purpose.

As a reader, you may not recognize Grassleaf's authors, but hopefully you will recognize our logo and trust that it represents a worthwhile work.

Grassleaf Publishing was created to do one thing: contribute a verse.

—Charles Brandon Wagoner

grassleaf
PUBLISHING

...contributing a verse.